Field Day for Eugene

Kindness, Acceptance, Inclusion

Written by
Maria Lei Antonio

Maria Lei Antonio

Illustrated by
Bonnie Lemaire

Halo
PUBLISHING
INTERNATIONAL

ISBN: 978-1-63765-077-6
LCCN: 2021913702

Halo Publishing International, LLC
www.halopublishing.com

Printed and bound in the United States of America

For Mom and Dad. Thank you. Your constant support and unending love are appreciated more than you'll ever know.

It was the first day of school. The warm breeze blew through the trees at Ross Elementary. Eugene and his friends were very excited for the new school year to begin. This year, Eugene and the rest of his classmates would be able to take part in field day.

Field day was a day when each class would compete against each other in all different kinds of games and activities. The class with the most points at the end of the day would win a large trophy and their picture would be displayed in the school's newsletter.

The months passed and Eugene's excitement grew each day. No class and a day spent with his friends sounded like fun to Eugene.

"I'm so excited for the water balloon toss. I've been practicing all summer with my sister, Lucy," he said to Ms. Grey.

The middle of June rolled around, and field day was right around the corner. Ms. Grey posted the list of games and activities at the front of the class so the students could see what they would be able to participate in. Kickball, water balloon toss, ring toss, tug of war, and a race on the track were just a few of the activities that were on the list.

"I can't wait," said Eugene eagerly.

A few days passed and field day was finally here. The class was thrilled for the day ahead. Ms. Grey gathered all the students to the carpet and explained that each activity was an opportunity for the students to work together as a team to earn points.

"How is Eugene going to participate? He is in a wheelchair. How is he going to run in the track race and play in the kickball game?" asked Henry.

Ms. Grey looked at Eugene. His face was sad. His eyes filled with tears. Eugene never thought about his wheelchair. He felt silly for thinking that he would be able to participate in field day.

Ms. Grey looked at the class and said, "Of course Eugene will be able to participate. Just because he is in a wheelchair doesn't mean he can't participate in the activities."

Eugene's head lifted.

"Eugene, you could roll the ball in kickball," said Lucile.

"And you can still participate in the track race using your wheelchair," said Sam.

"You can be my partner in the water balloon toss," said Catherine.

Eugene's face lit up with happiness. It was at that moment that Henry realized that Eugene could do all the same things that he could even though he was in a wheelchair. Eugene would just have to do things a little differently.

Throughout the day, each of the students participated in the various activities. Eugene was able to take part in all of them. He competed alongside Henry in the track race. He did the water balloon toss with Catherine, and he even rolled the ball in kickball. Everyone was having a blast.

15

At the end of field day, Mr. Wilson, the principal, gathered all the classes at the flagpole. Everyone waited anxiously for him to announce the winner.

"And the overall winner for the day is... Ms. Grey's third grade."

The class erupted with excitement.

When the students arrived back at their classroom, Ms. Grey looked at the final score sheet. To her surprise, she saw that the class had only won by one point. Her eyes scanned the score page until she saw that Eugene and Catherine had won the water balloon toss, putting the class one point ahead of all the others.

Later that day, she gathered the class and said, "I am so proud of all of you. You all are unique and have your own individual strengths that helped our class win today. Each of you are truly extraordinary!"

Amid the cheering, Ms. Grey's eyes locked with Eugene's. A tear formed and slid down her cheek. She was smiling and so was he.

It was at that moment that Eugene realized that even though he was different from those around him, he was still capable of amazing things. He knew that he would never let his wheelchair keep him from doing the things that others could do. Eugene knew that from here on out, he would always be unstoppable, for he knew he was fearfully and wonderfully made.

CPSIA information can be obtained
at www.ICGtesting.com
Printed in the USA
JSHW050811120222
22695JS00011B/135